Hoglet
the Spineless Hedgehog

Hoglet
the Spineless
Hedgehog

Allyson Marnoch
Illustrated by Lorraine Ward

 Kelpies

For Brian, Roy and Emma

Kelpies is an imprint of Floris Books

First published in 2007 as *H's Second Chance*
by Allyson Marnoch
This edition published in 2010 by Floris Books

Text © 1999, 2010 Allyson Marnoch
Illustrations © 2007, 2010 Lorraine Ward

The publisher acknowledges a Lottery grant from
the Scottish Arts Council towards the publication
of this imprint.

British Library CIP Data available
ISBN 978-086315-742-4
Printed in Poland

Contents

1. A Late Litter 9
2. A Homeless Hog 22
3. An Icy Situation 33
4. A Nasty Incident 45
5. Haggis or Hedgehog? 56
6. A Glimmer of Hope 61
7. Horribly Lost 70
8. Egg on Legs 80
9. Baxter Lends a Helping Horn ... 85
10. Don't Roll Up! 95
11. Hope at Last 98
12. A Warming Tail 112
13. Hedgehog Heaven 120
14. Spring 127
    Hog Epilogue 133

Where will you go my spiky wee friend
When the cold winds start to blow?
What will you eat, where will you sleep,
When the ground is white with snow?

Roll up tight and say goodnight,
Dream the cold away,
Wait till spring, in a prickly ball,
For a warm and sunny day.

1. A Late Litter

The trees were bare in Tumbly Wood. Their fallen leaves covered the ground with rich shades of red, orange and gold. It was a beautiful sight, but one which signalled the end of autumn and the arrival of winter.

In her small nest, made using twigs, leaves and heather, a mother hedgehog tried to protect her newly born babies from the icy wind that howled across Finbrae Estate in the Scottish Highlands.

"Well," Mrs Hog said, looking at her

offspring, "it's not the best time of year for you to have been born, but you all look healthy." She checked each baby thoroughly as they slept. "As long as I can feed you up well enough before the snow arrives, I think you'll make grand hedgehogs," she added. And with that she curled up beside them and fell fast asleep.

For the first week or so everything was fine. The babies fed well and each day they became stronger and bigger. By the end of the second week, all but one of them had opened their eyes. Mrs Hog had already noticed that the fourth baby was the last to do everything. He seemed to be smaller than the rest, but what worried her more than anything was that he had no spines.

"Oh dear," she said. "Perhaps it would be

kinder if I let nature take its course. Perhaps I should stop feeding him and that would be that." Suddenly, just as she was finishing her sentence, the little creature gave a gigantic yawn and opened his eyes wide for the very first time. He looked curiously around him. "Oh my goodness, you've got eyes like saucers!" exclaimed his mother.

Each night, before the babies woke up, Mrs Hog peered closely at her smallest child's tough skin, hoping to see spines appearing. But each time, to her dismay, he was completely bald.

There was no time to waste before Mrs Hog started to teach her babies how to forage for food themselves. So, when they were four weeks old, she decided to take them out on their first expedition into the woods.

I'll have to name them before I take them out, she thought to herself, *so that I don't lose them.* She looked at the four little creatures, who were still fast asleep.

The biggest hoglet was feisty and looked as though he might be adventurous. "I'm going to name you Horatio," she decided. The second and third hoglets were both girls. "I think Heather would suit you," she said to the second one. "And you're so spiky," she said, pricking her nose on the third youngster, "that I'm going to call you Holly."

But when she came to the fourth child, she stopped smiling. "Oh dear little thing, how ever will you survive without spines?" Mrs Hog knew that a hedgehog without spines would have little chance of survival, and she didn't give names to the hoglets she knew would probably not survive on their own. She looked at his huge, innocent eyes and little turned-up nose and after a minute or so she said, "Nature can be cruel. I'm sure winter is going to be hard this year, and I just don't know what will happen to this little fellow. This is the eighth litter I've had and I've named each litter alphabetically starting with 'A', so ..." she turned back to the tiny hedgehog, "your name will have to start with 'H'. I think I'll call you Hoglet."

It was dusk and the time had arrived for the youngsters' first expedition. Before leaving the safety of the nest Mrs Hog gathered them together. "Tonight," she said, "I'm going to teach you how to find water and where to look for woodlice and worms. Stay close to me at all times and don't go wandering off."

The little group set out. Mrs Hog in front, followed by Horatio, Heather, Holly and last of all, and probably a little bit further behind than he should have been, little Hoglet.

They scuttled from bush to bush through leaves so deep that, at some points, they reached their shoulders. Horatio and his sisters thought this was

great fun and giggled as the leaves stuck to their spines, but Hoglet didn't enjoy it much; his bare skin just felt cold and damp. He was glad when their mother guided them to a small clearing where the branches of the trees hung low and it felt warm and welcoming. The wind howled viciously through the rest of the wood but the huge oaks stood firm against the raging gusts while the three youngsters rummaged among the leaves for something to eat.

It had rained earlier in the day so there was no problem finding water. "Always look for a dock leaf or a piece of hollowed-out tree," advised their mother. "There's nearly always water there. If it hasn't been raining, head down to the bottom of the wood and you'll find a wee loch."

Next she poked an old piece of wood aside with her snout. "Woodlice and beetles tend to live under pieces of rotten logs," she said, and released a string of woodlice in the direction of her hungry children. "Eat up," she smiled, "and then we'll go home."

The hoglets were tired and cold after their outing, and very happy to return to the comfort of the nest. But while his brother and sisters curled up in a large bundle, making them look rather like

one huge hedgehog, little Hoglet slept all alone in a corner. It wasn't that he didn't love his brother and sisters; he would have liked to have joined them, but they were just too prickly and he found it rather painful to cuddle up against them.

Horatio became impatient and was keen to leave the nest. "You may leave tomorrow," said his mother. "You'll be six weeks old and I've taught you all I know. But don't forget ... nature can be hard.

Only the fittest survive and it can be tough fending for yourself, especially at this time of year." She looked at Hoglet. He was the only member of the litter who wasn't looking excited about leaving home. In fact, he looked rather worried. "Don't worry, Hoglet," she said, "I'm sure you'll be fine."

The last day in the safety of their mother's warm nest passed far too quickly for Hoglet. As dusk fell that evening, it was time for the youngsters to leave. "Now, remember everything I've told you," said their mother. "Be on your guard at all times — you won't get a second chance. You're animals — only humans get a second chance."

"There's one more thing I must tell you before you go," she said. "It's going to be a really bad winter. In a few weeks, the cold will make you feel sleepy and it will be time to start hibernating over the winter months. You must find somewhere safe to make a nest, and you must put on enough weight so you'll have plenty of

fat to live off until the spring. Otherwise, you won't wake up from hibernation."

Horatio and his two sisters didn't worry about this final piece of advice. They were already quite plump after their foraging expeditions. But Hoglet hadn't managed to find much to eat and was still rather small. His brothers and sisters couldn't contain themselves any longer and ran off into the woods, all on the look out for beetles and slugs. "Don't forget to be polite," their mother called after them. "Have a Spiky Day!"

Hoglet shuffled hesitantly from foot to foot in the doorway of the nest. "Well, I'll be going then," he said reluctantly.

"Goodbye, little one," said his mother. "Be brave."

"Goodbye, Mum. Have a Spiky Day," he said.

Mrs Hog watched as her fourth child toddled away aimlessly. A large tear rolled down her snout before she turned and went back into her nest.

2. A Homeless Hog

Hoglet didn't really know where he was going. It was already dark and with his bare skin and no spines to protect him, he could feel that it was getting colder. He had half hoped that he might bump into Horatio or one of his sisters, but there was no sign of them. *I expect they're miles away by now,* he thought.

He decided he should really look for some food, but first he needed a drink. It hadn't rained for several days and he couldn't find any water in the wood. He remembered what his mother had said about the loch ... but where was it?

He found a little track and shuffled his way along, deep in concentration, with his snout to the ground. The strong winds, which had blasted Finbrae Estate over the last few days, had blown many branches from the trees and these were now scattered everywhere. Hoglet kept getting his little paws stuck between them.

"Oh dear," he said, stopping for a minute under the cover of a gigantic toadstool. "Perhaps I should have gone a different way."

"Well, I for one, wish you *had* gone a different way!"

The high-pitched voice startled Hoglet and he jumped backwards, feeling his bare skin rub against the clammy root of the toadstool.

He looked up but couldn't see anyone. He turned round in a big circle, but there was still no one to be seen.

"Now I'll have to build it all over again," continued the voice.

Hoglet peered hard into the darkness when, to his surprise, he saw a large, spotty spider hanging from a long piece of web.

"Oh hello," he said. "What will you have to build again?"

"My house," said the spider. "You've just walked right through it."

"I'm so sorry, I didn't mean to. I didn't see it."

"Never mind," said the spider. "Webs can be very difficult to see, especially at night. Spiders are used to having to renovate their homes all the time. Humans are always destroying them and if you're a house spider, people attack you with feather dusters. And they have these slippery things in their homes called 'baths'. Several of my relatives have been caught in them — it's awful. That's why I came to live in Tumbly Wood — I thought it might be safer."

"I was looking for some water," said Hoglet. "Do you know where I might find some?"

"Well, the loch's not far from here. It's

that way," said the spider, pointing in eight different directions at once.

"Thank you so much," said Hoglet, looking confused but remembering to be polite. "I'm sorry again about your home."

"It doesn't matter," replied the spider. "The weather's getting so cold that I don't think I'll be catching any food in my web until next year now."

Despite the spider's directions, Hoglet found the loch, and after a long drink and catching a few earthworms beside the path, he headed back towards the middle of the wood. It was already starting to get light and he had to find somewhere quiet and safe to sleep for the day. He searched around for some time, before he finally decided to settle in the large hollow of an old tree. It felt safe and was lined with moss. "This'll do fine," he said. "No prickly bits to scratch my skin." He'd had a busy night and within a few minutes he was curled up on his mossy bed, in a deep sleep.

Hoglet was in the middle of a wonderful dream: he'd grown spines — loads of them, all over his back — and he'd met up with Horatio, Heather and Holly. They were in the wood playing a game together with pine cones, shoving them with their snouts to see who could push theirs furthest.

He was suddenly awoken by a clunking noise, followed by another and then another. He opened one eye sleepily and began to unroll himself. He couldn't understand what was going on. It seemed to be raining hazelnuts! They were falling through the centre of the tree. A red squirrel poked his nose down through the hollow trunk.

"Whoops ... sorry! Did I hit you?" he asked.

"Yes, you did actually," replied Hoglet. "What were you doing?"

"Well, I'm afraid you've fallen asleep in my store cupboard," said the squirrel.

"Oh dear, I had no idea it belonged to anyone. It's just that I'm so tired and I needed somewhere warm and quiet to curl up for the day."

"What type of animal are you anyway?" asked the squirrel.

"I'm a hedgehog," said Hoglet.

The squirrel laughed. "Are you *sure?*" he asked.

Hoglet looked down at the ground, a bit embarrassed. "I am *definitely* a hedgehog," he replied.

"Aren't you supposed to have spines then?" the squirrel asked.

"Yes," said Hoglet sadly, "but I don't seem to have any."

"Well, I wouldn't worry about it. Worrying won't solve anything. I can see you've got goosebumps on your skin though," said the squirrel, leaning further over the edge of the trunk to get a better view of Hoglet. "Maybe some spines will pop out from them soon."

"Maybe," sighed Hoglet, not sounding convinced.

"You're very welcome to stay here longer if you want," said the squirrel, "but that hollow will soon be full of nuts for my winter stash. I've got to make sure they're well hidden or the grey squirrels will pinch them and I'll starve to death. It's going to be a very bad winter this year," he added.

"Yes, I've heard," sighed Hoglet, remembering what his mother and the spider had said about the bad weather that was on its way. He knew that if he was going to survive this awful winter that all the woodland creatures kept talking about, he was going to have to put on some weight very quickly.

"If it's all right with you, could I stay until darkness falls tonight? Then I'll be on my way." asked Hoglet hopefully.

"Of course," replied the squirrel. "I'll let you get back to sleep," and he hopped back up the tree, burbling to himself, "So much to do ... so little time ..."

Hoglet curled himself up in a tight, miserable ball and worried about what was going to happen to him, before dropping off to sleep.

3. An Icy Situation

As night fell, Hoglet left the safety of the tree stump. It was cold and the moon cast a pale glow over Tumbly Wood. The cold air was making him feel very hungry so he decided to look for something to eat. He wandered around for hours looking for a meal, but it seemed that when it was cold all the insects stayed well hidden. Even the famous Scottish midges seemed to have disappeared.

"Oh, I'm *so* hungry and I feel as if I've been walking for miles," groaned Hoglet.

He went a little further, and had almost
given up any hope of finding anything
to eat when he spotted a huge slug lying
right in the middle of the path. Hoglet's

mouth began to water as the moonlight shone over the slug's enormous glistening body.

"That looks *delicious!*" he exclaimed. He started to move towards the slug, but stopped dead in his tracks as a resounding *CRACK* echoed through the otherwise silent wood. He dashed back under the safety of a fern and peered around cautiously, his heart beating faster and faster as the minutes ticked by. He couldn't see anything. He couldn't hear anything. The silence returned.

It must have been an old branch breaking off one of the trees, thought Hoglet, trying to reassure himself. He scampered forward quietly, checking around him again, but there was nothing to be seen. But there was *someone* there: someone who was very good at blending into the branches;

someone with very good eyesight, even at night; someone who could keep absolutely still, but still move his head almost all the way round. "Someone" was an owl. A Scottish tawny owl to be precise, and he was very, very hungry.

Hoglet was about to take his first bite of the juicy slug when a screech and a hideous flapping noise came from the moonlit sky. He saw the owl swoop towards him and rolled himself into a tight ball. But it was pointless. He felt the creature's huge talons sink into his skin and heard the powerful flapping of the bird's strong wings lifting him higher and higher into the cold night sky. Hoglet started to wriggle and gasp as the air was squeezed from his tiny body. Thinking all was lost, he shut his eyes tightly, preparing himself for his fate, but

instead he found himself falling through the air. Had his wriggling set him free? Or had the owl spotted a tastier meal? He didn't know, but he was happy to have an unexpectedly soft landing in a large patch of thistles.

The scared little hedgehog stayed there, stiff and uncomfortable, hoping the bird wouldn't return. He watched through a gap in the thistles as it circled a few times and eventually disappeared. Hoglet squeaked quietly as the thistles cut into his delicate skin and he tried to lick the wound the owl had left on his back. Although it wasn't the most comfortable of beds, he decided he would just have to stay in his prickly surroundings until the morning.

As the sun rose the following day, Hoglet was happy to leave the uncomfortable thistle bed he'd been hiding in. He was cold and hungry, not to mention tired and thirsty, so he decided he would go down to the loch to forage, have a drink and see if some water might soothe the wound the owl had left on his back. He was more careful this time, darting from bush to bush, keeping under cover all the time.

"At least I know the way to the loch now," he said to himself. But something was wrong. There was a hard, crisp feeling in the air. Hoglet could hardly feel his four paws and for some reason everything looked white and crunchy. As he walked through the leaves, he noticed he left small paw marks behind him.

He soon arrived at the water's edge, but to his surprise there was no water.

"That's strange," he said. "What's happened to all the water? It's gone all hard and sparkly."

Hoglet tried dipping one of his paws into the water, but instead of making a gentle ripple, it made a tapping sound.

"Something's definitely wrong," said Hoglet. "Water isn't meant to be hard."

He moved a little closer to the loch but, seconds later, Hoglet found that his paws were moving in different directions and he was sliding uncontrollably.

"Help!" he cried. "I can't stop! What's happening?" He scrabbled furiously with his feet, but the more effort he made, the faster he seemed to move across the ice towards the centre of the loch.

Before he had time to say anything else, Hoglet slid off the ice which had formed around the edge of the loch, and found himself gasping to catch his breath as he hit the icy cold water. He'd never tried swimming before and as the freezing water bit into his tiny body he found it harder and harder to move.

Hoglet's head seemed to be under the water as much as above it now, but as he took a final gasp of air and looked around him for what he thought would be the last time, he spotted a log just a few feet away from him. Knowing it was his only chance, he scrambled towards it and managed to clamber on top and out of the freezing water. He did his best not to shiver, as every movement of his shaking body made the log wobble.

"Oh no," he squealed, "it's all very well floating here, but I'll never be able to swim back to dry land."

This is it, I'm going to drown. I survived an attack by an owl last night only to drown in this awful loch, he thought to himself.

Hoglet knew that if he fell in again, he probably wouldn't survive. He sat absolutely still, wondering what to do next. He was floating, but completely stranded in the middle of the loch.

In the distance Hoglet heard the sound of dogs barking and horses running on frozen turf. As the noise grew he also heard a panting sound. He looked around carefully, trying not to wobble the log too much. It was a hunt and he could see a fox running for its life, heading straight for the water. Hoglet watched in amazement as the creature took a massive leap into the icy cold loch. It didn't seem to notice Hoglet, but swam straight past him, not stopping until it got to the other side where it lay exhausted.

The barking kept coming closer and closer until the dogs came into view.

A few of them ran into the water, but decided it was far too chilly and ran back quickly onto dry land. Then out of nowhere a large fat man, with a face as red as his jacket, appeared from the edge of the wood on horseback. He didn't seem to notice the loch as he drove his horse onwards. The horse, however, had seen the water and decided it was not going to get wet. It dug its hooves into

the ground and juddered to a halt so suddenly that the large man flew over the horse's ears to land with an almighty splash, slap-bang in the middle of the icy water.

As he did so, Hoglet's little log was caught by an enormous wave and he and the log were thrown back onto dry land. Hoglet let go of the log and shut his eyes tightly as he flew through the air. He landed with a gentle thump in a deep, soft thicket of heather. He didn't dare open his eyes and just stayed rolled up in a ball — a very *tight* ball.

4. A Nasty Incident

Hoglet could hear the dogs being told to go home. And the fat man was obviously cross, as the rest of the huntsmen were laughing at him. The little hedgehog kept absolutely still until the noise of the humans and the hunt died away.

When he was sure they had gone, he began to unroll very slowly and carefully opened one eye then the other, but to his horror he found himself face to face with the fox.

Hoglet gulped. He remembered his

mother had said that foxes were very dangerous. A determined fox would eat a hedgehog. He wanted to run but he knew there was no point. He was too cold to move anyway. All he could do was shiver.

"Hello," gasped the fox, still trying to get his breath back.

"Hello," said Hoglet timidly.

"What's your name then?" asked the fox.

"I'm Hoglet."

The fox looked amused. "Is that a real name?"

"It's *my* name," the hedgehog replied. "Are you going to eat me?"

"Why on earth would I want to do that?" asked the fox.

"Because I'm a hedgehog."

"Are you?" The fox looked at Hoglet more closely. "I thought hedgehogs were supposed to be prickly."

"They are, but I don't have any spines," explained Hoglet miserably.

"Don't worry," said the fox. "You can relax. If I wasn't so exhausted then I *might* eat you, but I've been chased by that hunt for quite some distance and I'm far too tired at the moment."

"I thought fox-hunting had been banned," said Hoglet innocently.

"Oh, it has!" answered the fox, "and now that it has been outlawed, you'd have thought that life would be a bit easier. But every so often those silly hounds decide that real foxes smell better than the scent trail, so we still get chased! Not a bad day though," the fox went on. "I've been waiting for something horrible to happen to that fat chap. Do you know ... he's been chasing me and my family for years, despite the hunting ban! Maybe he'll think twice after his little swim."

The fox grinned, stood up and shook all the water from his coat. "Well, I'll be on my way then," he said. "I must find something to eat. Goodbye."

"Bye then," said Hoglet.

The fox trotted off, leaving Hoglet shivering at the edge of the loch. The wound on his back was still bleeding, and he was hungry and starting to look thin.

The fox had only gone a few yards when he turned round and called to the hedgehog, "You're not going to stay there, are you? You'll be eaten by an eagle or something if you're not careful. There's a bad winter on the way and plenty of birds of prey around here who would happily make a meal out of you. They've all got good appetites, you know, and the colder it gets, the hungrier they become."

"Actually ..." said Hoglet, looking a bit embarrassed, "I haven't really thought about where to go."

"What you mean is that you haven't *got* anywhere to go," corrected the fox.

"No, you're right, I haven't," Hoglet admitted.

"You'd better come with me then. I'm off to Wheatley Farm, and I know just the place where you'll be able to rest and get warm. I can show you where to find some cracked hens' eggs, too, if you like."

"That would be wonderful," said Hoglet, cheering up at the thought of food.

It didn't take Hoglet and the fox long to reach the farm; the fox knew all the short cuts.

"Right, now that we're here, we'd better split up," the fox said. "The hen house is over there and there are always a few cracked eggs lying around. Just be careful the farmer doesn't see you. Good luck!"

"Thanks for not eating me," said Hoglet shyly, "and for all your help."

"You're welcome," said the fox. "Now hurry. Go and find something to eat."

There was a small hatch leading into the hen house and Hoglet had become so thin that he fitted through it easily. None of the hens noticed his arrival as

an argument seemed to have broken out between a large Scots Dumpy called Martha and a small White Silkie named Thelma, as to who had laid the biggest egg that day. Hoglet spotted four cracked eggs lying on the floor and quietly ate two of them while the argument continued. It felt good to have his tummy full again and it was so warm in the hen house that he decided to stay there a bit longer. He would leave the farm and head back to Tumbly Wood early in the morning, just before daylight.

Very quietly, after a good sleep, and feeling a little better after eating the other two eggs, Hoglet crept out of the little house as quietly as he had arrived. It wasn't far to the edge of the wood but he knew he would have to be careful as he crossed the farmyard.

"I doubt if there are any humans awake yet," Hoglet said to himself, peeping out from behind a pile of old bricks. He couldn't see anyone so he scuttled off as fast as he could. But halfway across the yard he smelled a wonderful smell that made his mouth water. Try as he might, he just couldn't resist it. He had to find out what it was.

He discovered that the source of the lovely smell was some scraps of food on a plate near the farmhouse door. Hoglet ran up to it and started eating. It was so delicious that he completely forgot where he was. Suddenly he heard footsteps behind him. He turned and saw a huge farmer charging towards him with a big, rusty spade.

"I'll get you, you big rat!" he yelled.

Hoglet wanted so much to roll up into

a ball, but he knew that wouldn't help. The farmer had mistaken him for a rat! He remembered his mother's last words as he had left the nest — "Be brave" — so he ran. He ran as fast as his legs would carry him, but that wasn't quite fast enough. The farmer's fourth blow at little Hoglet caught him on one of his back legs. It was agony but still he kept running and managed to reach the safety of an old barn. He ran in between two bales of straw and stayed absolutely still, hardly daring to breathe and trying not to squeal.

"Filthy rat! I'll get you!" the farmer shouted, but after pacing up and down the barn for a few minutes, he left.

Hoglet turned round and had a look at his leg. It was bleeding and he couldn't move it. He pushed himself further into the straw and pondered what he should do next, before deciding he would just have to stay where he was for the rest of the day.

5. Haggis or Hedgehog?

As darkness fell Hoglet decided he would try again to leave Wheatley Farm.

He stood at the barn door and sniffed the air. It was starting to freeze. He didn't have far to go and was keen to get back to Tumbly Wood and as far away as possible from the farmer and his big spade. His leg was numb now and it dragged behind him when he walked.

He was just about to crouch under the farm gates when he saw two huge green eyes glinting in front of him, attached to a muscular body with thick, striped, greyish fur, and a luxurious tail. Hoglet froze. It was a Scottish wildcat. Its yellowed fangs hung menacingly over its black lips, and strings of drool slid to the ground as it opened its mouth.

"What do you think you're up to?" hissed the creature.

"N ... nothing ..." stammered Hoglet. "I'm just trying to get home."

"What are you doing on the farm?" asked the wildcat.

"Finding food," said Hoglet, "eating a few broken eggs. Nobody seemed to want them."

"That's stealing," said the wildcat. "I have to catch mice and rats and things if I want to eat. In fact, now that I look at you, you look a bit like a rat. Or ..." the creature laughed, revealing long, sharp teeth, "maybe you're a haggis with legs! What on earth *are* you? I've never seen anything like you before!"

"I'm not a rat or a haggis," explained Hoglet, quite offended and with no idea what a haggis was. "I'm a hedgehog," he said proudly.

"Oh, that's a good one," snarled the cat. "Do you think I'm daft or something?"

"But I *am* a hedgehog ... honestly!"

protested Hoglet. "I just haven't got any spines."

"Oh, don't be so ridiculous. Whoever heard of such a thing?" taunted the cat.

"It does happen sometimes," said Hoglet sadly.

"What are you called then?" asked the wildcat.

"Hoglet."

"Hoglet?" repeated the wildcat. "That's not a proper name. A bald hedgehog called Hoglet? It's my guess that your mother didn't think you would survive in the wild, so she didn't bother giving you a proper name. Now push off and don't come back here again. If your skin didn't look like a piece of leather I'd have you for breakfast."

Hoglet was just about to pluck up enough courage to explain to the wildcat that his mother couldn't have thought that, or she wouldn't have named him at all, when without any warning the creature lashed out with its sharp claws and shoved him along the path. Hoglet rolled up as tightly as he could. He rolled and rolled until he thought he was never going to stop, before coming to rest with a bump at the foot of an old oak tree.

6. A Glimmer of Hope

Hoglet's skin was bleeding badly and the cold wind was biting into him. He didn't know exactly where he was going, but at least he was back in Tumbly Wood. He limped along aimlessly, squeaking in pain every time he dragged his back leg.

All of a sudden he heard "ahtisshoo!" and at the same time a blackcurrant came flying out from a bush and hit him on the head. Hoglet stuck his nose inside the bush to find that it wasn't really a bush at all, but a hollowed-out log. It was covered in brambles, looked warm and dry, and inside was a tiny field mouse.

"I'm sorry, did that blackcurrant hit you?" she asked.

"Yes, but I'm so battered and bruised that it doesn't matter any more," he said sadly. "It didn't hurt anyway," he added.

"I've got this awful cold," explained the mouse in a squeaky voice, "and I

sneezed and the currant flew out of my mouth. Aren't you going to come in?" she asked.

"Oh yes, please," said Hoglet.

"Goodness me," said the mouse, looking closely at Hoglet. "You are in a bad way, aren't you? Here, have a currant. What happened to you?"

Hoglet told the mouse all about the owl, nearly drowning in the loch, the farmer and the wildcat. A large tear ran down his little snout and landed with a plop in the small pile of fruit the mouse had been collecting.

"Have you got any brothers and sisters?" she asked.

"Yes," said Hoglet, suddenly realising how much he missed them.

"And did *they* all have spines?" continued the mouse.

"Oh yes," said Hoglet proudly. "Horatio, my brother, is really big and spiky and I have two sisters, Heather and Holly. My mother named Holly after a holly bush because she's so prickly," he explained. "But when it came to me she just gave me the name Hoglet. Perhaps that horrible wildcat was right. Perhaps she didn't want to name me properly because she didn't think I'd survive. Now winter's coming and I'm too thin to hibernate, and I can't find anywhere to sleep anyway."

"So what you're saying," said the mouse, "is that you want to be able to hibernate safely all winter?"

"Well, yes," said Hoglet, "but what I'd really like, more than anything, is to have my own spines so that I can be independent ... and I'd really like a proper name as well," he added.

"Well," said the mouse, "in that case, you need to find Second Chance House. There's a human there who'll help you."

"A human?" repeated Hoglet. "But my mother told me that humans are bad."

"Not *all* humans are bad," explained the mouse, sneezing again. "Some of them can be very kind."

"But what's Second Chance House?" asked the hedgehog.

"Second Chance House is the house where Margaret Love lives. It's not far from here ... it's on the Finbrae Estate. She takes in injured animals, nurses them back to health and then releases them once they're fit and healthy."

"That sounds wonderful," said Hoglet longingly, "but how do I get there?"

"Listen hard," said the mouse, "and I'll tell you."

Hoglet paid careful attention as the tiny mouse gave him "smelling" directions to Second Chance House. "It's not far," she said, "but there is a road to cross so you'll need to be careful. Leave the wood and head for the north edge of Tumbly Meadow. The farmer's just

ploughed the soil so you'll be able to smell it. Cut through the field until you smell some pigs — that'll be easy," she giggled. "After that, turn left into an ostrich farm and shortly beyond the ostriches you should smell milk from the dairy ... the cows are Highland cows by the way, so they're very large with horns and long hair."

"Soil, pigs, ostriches and Highland cattle," repeated Hoglet.

"Finally, and this is the most dangerous part," warned the mouse, "you'll come to a busy road. Once you've crossed the road, go down a short lane and on the right-hand side you'll see a long driveway lined with Scots Pine trees. At the end of that drive is Second Chance House."

"Oh gosh. I hope I can remember all that," said Hoglet.

"I'm sure you will," said the mouse. "You have to ... it's your only chance."

Hoglet was excited at the thought of Second Chance House. So excited in fact, that he forgot how weak he was and that he wouldn't be able to walk far with his injured leg.

"Why don't you wait until it's dark tomorrow evening?" suggested the mouse. "You're welcome to stay here."

"That's very kind of you," said Hoglet, remembering his manners.

So Hoglet spent that night and the following day repeating the list of smelling directions in his head over and over again.

At last, the time came for him to leave his tiny friend. "Thanks for everything," he said. "I hope your cold gets better."

"Good luck!" squeaked the mouse.

"Soil, pigs, ostriches, Highland cattle, road, lane, Scots Pines," repeated Hoglet as he shuffled off in the direction of Tumbly Meadow. He reached the north edge of the field and took a long, deep breath.

"Yes, I can smell soil," he said. His leg was hurting and the skin on his back was cracked and bleeding, but at least he was now hopeful of finding somewhere to spend the winter. He felt much happier.

7. Horribly Lost

Having walked across the field of freshly ploughed soil, Hoglet stopped again and looked around.

"Next I've got to smell pigs," he said to himself, but as he stood at the edge of the field a thick, damp fog started to fill the air, making it impossible to smell anything.

"Oh no," cried Hoglet, starting to panic. He could smell something and wasn't quite sure what it was.

"Well, I can't stay here all night anyway,"

he said, so he followed his nose, but soon found himself at the entrance to a rabbit warren. A head with two large teeth appeared at the hole.

"Hello!" said the rabbit. "What and who are you?"

"I'm a hedgehog and my name's Hoglet ... but I haven't got any spines," he said.

"Oh!" said the rabbit. "That's unusual."

"Would you mind if I came in?" asked Hoglet.

"Well, if you had spines then I *would* mind," said the rabbit, "because you'd hurt all my brothers and sisters, but seeing as you're bald, you're very welcome."

"Thank you," said Hoglet, thinking that for once it was useful *not* to be prickly.

He looked up and down the maze of dark tunnels. Several more heads popped up from more holes, said "hello," then disappeared again.

"Shouldn't you be hibernating?" asked the rabbit.

"I can't find anywhere in the wood and I'm not really fat enough just yet," said Hoglet, and he went on to explain how he had been on his way to Second Chance House when the fog had come down and he'd lost his way.

"Never heard of it myself," said the rabbit. "Hang on, I'll ask my wife." And with that he turned and yelled down the tunnel. "Anyone know the way to Second Chance House?"

No fewer than eleven little heads popped out of eleven holes. "It's that way," they said, all pointing in different directions. Hoglet sighed and decided that the rabbits, just like the spider, were only going to confuse him if he stayed much longer. So he thanked them all and left the warren.

The fog wasn't just grey now, but yellow and so thick it was impossible to see where he was going. Cold and miserable once again, Hoglet wandered on until he found some long grass to rest in until the weather cleared.

As daylight arrived the fog lifted, but it was still cold. Hoglet unrolled himself and peered out carefully from the grass.

"Oh no!" he cried. "I'm at Tumbly Loch. I've spent the night going round in a big circle." He curled up in the grass and sobbed.

"What's up?" asked a robin, landing beside him.

In between sobs, Hoglet told the robin that he was trying to find Second Chance House and how much he'd been looking forward to going there.

"I'm useless," he said. "I don't think I deserve to survive any more."

"Nonsense!" chirped the robin. "I can tell you all about Second Chance House.

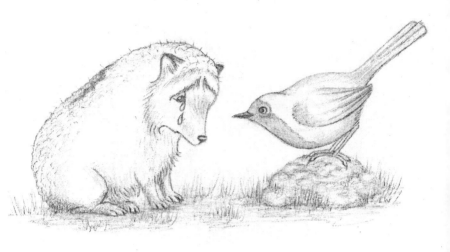

I go there myself as a matter of fact. It's owned by a lady called Margaret Love, who loves animals. When it gets really cold and hard to find food in the wood, I fly over to her house and she feeds me. She's so kind that she even buys special robin food for me ... it's got grub worms in it. The collared doves get pinhead oatmeal, which is *their* favourite, the blue tits are given as many unsalted peanuts as they can possibly eat, and she chops up bread and apples for the blackbirds. She even kept some leftover haggis and neeps on Burns' Night for us. I must admit, I wasn't too keen on it, but the family of mice who live in a flowerpot in her garden shed ate so much of it I thought they were going to explode! She knows all about hedgehogs, too, by the way; she rescued a lot of them from the Isle of Uist last year and brought them to her garden.

"The good thing is," continued the robin, "that she really doesn't live that far from here. Her house is only about a mile away as the crow flies."

"As the crow flies?" repeated Hoglet. "But you're a robin, aren't you?"

"Yes," laughed the robin, "but *as the crow flies* is just an expression people use.

It's the shortest distance between two points."

"Oh, I see," said Hoglet, still feeling a little muddled. "Do you think you could help me get there?" he asked hopefully.

"Of course I can. The only problem will be the road," said the robin.

"Yes, I know," said Hoglet. "The mouse warned me about the road as well."

"How far did you get last night?" asked the robin.

"I reached the edge of the field that's just been ploughed, and I was heading off towards the pigs when that awful fog came down," said Hoglet.

"If I were you," said the robin, "I wouldn't bother about smelling everything; the fog has lifted now so you'll see all the landmarks as you come to them. Once you reach the Highland cattle, you'll be able to see the road from their field. After you've crossed the road you just have to go along a lane and there's a row of large Scots Pine trees leading up to Second Chance House. Why don't you have a drink and set off now?" suggested the little bird. "If you travel all day you should be there by tonight."

Hoglet thought about this. He shouldn't really be out during the daytime, but he was desperate to reach the safety of Margaret Love's house.

"The weather's getting worse," persuaded the robin.

"Yes, you're probably right," said Hoglet decisively. "I'll leave now."

So after a final drink from Tumbly Loch, Hoglet set off on his journey again, shuffling as best he could through the cold, crisp leaves. The air was clear, but it was very cold and he was sure he could smell snow close by. "No time to waste," he said to himself. "I must keep going."

8. Egg on Legs

It was easy to see the pigs when he reached the edge of the field, but with his bad leg and scratched skin, it took Hoglet all morning to reach the ostrich farm. He had never seen an ostrich before and only knew what the large birds were because the mouse had explained that they had long legs and big bottoms.

"Goodness me! What huge eggs they lay," he said. "I wonder if I can find one that's cracked." In one corner of the field there was a large shed that the farmer had built for the ostriches. Hoglet went inside the warm, comfortable building. A thick layer of straw and soft wood shavings covered the floor.

"Perhaps I should just have a snooze before going any further," he said and decided to curl up for an hour or so and leave again when darkness fell. He closed his eyes and was sound asleep within minutes.

But Hoglet must have been more tired than he'd realised. He woke up with a start and scuttled to the door of the ostrich house. It was beginning to get dark outside. That didn't bother him, but what did bother him was the fact that it had begun to snow ... *heavily.*

He was standing in the doorway, trying to work out what to do, when one of the ostriches started running towards him.

Instinctively, he rolled himself into a tight ball, then felt the large bird rolling him back carefully into the middle of the shed. The ostrich proceeded to scrape up some straw, gathered it round him and sat on top of him!

"Oh no! She thinks I'm one of her eggs," cried Hoglet. The bird didn't feel heavy; in fact, Hoglet had to admit that it was rather cosy, but he was anxious to get on with the next stage of his journey before the snow became any thicker.

He tried wriggling out from under the huge bird's feather skirt but it was no good; every time he moved, the bird gently pushed him back into position with her beak and readjusted her feathers. There was nothing Hoglet could do other than sit quietly in his feather prison, listening to the wind howling outside. Hours passed by and then he felt the ostrich becoming restless. She stood up and shook her massive feather skirt, sending straw and wood shavings through the air.

It's now or never, thought Hoglet, unrolling himself. He scuttled across to the door as fast as he could, leaving the ostrich rummaging in the straw, looking for her "egg on legs!"

9. Baxter Lends a Helping Horn

As he reached the doorway of the ostrich house and looked outside, Hoglet let out a little squeal of despair. It had been snowing the whole time he had been captured by the ostrich, and the snow lay deeper than he could ever have imagined in a thick white blanket. All the grass had been covered and the only thing visible was a huge boulder, which sat a short distance from the ostriches' house.

"What on earth am I going to do?"

he cried. "I'll never be able to reach Margaret Love now. I'm going to die."

Hoglet remembered what his mother had told him about snow. "There are two different types," she had said. "There is the hard, crunchy type which, if you're not too heavy, you can walk on. Then there's the powdery type, which can be carried for miles by the wind."

Hoglet stood on the ramp of the ostrich house, trying to decide whether the snow was crunchy or powdery. Hearing a thumping sound coming up behind him, he turned to see the over-friendly ostrich heading in his direction.

"Oh no! Not again!" he wailed as he jumped safely out of the clutches of the giant bird. Hoglet lay absolutely still on the surface of the snow and watched the ostrich retreat into the house.

It didn't take long before his four paws were numb, and the only way he could move was by wriggling along the surface of the snow like a huge worm.

After much wriggling and using up more energy than he had, Hoglet reached the boulder and lay on top of it, exhausted. Tired and weary, he closed

his eyes while a tear ran down his nose and melted a tiny patch of snow.

"Can I help you?" came a voice from above him.

Hoglet opened his tear-filled eyes to find himself staring into the eyes of an enormous Highland cow. Each time she breathed, warm air came from her gigantic nose, bringing life back into his frozen limbs.

"It's very kind of you to ask," he replied, "but no one can help me now. I was on my way to reach Margaret Love ... she's the only person who can help. She lives at Second Chance House you see, but now that the snow's come down I'm stuck on this boulder and I don't know what to do."

"I'm Hattie," said the Highland cow. "I'm sure my relatives can help you somehow or ..." Just as Hattie was finishing her sentence, a huge gust of wind blew off the hills and Hoglet toppled off the boulder, landing with a soft *plop* in the surrounding snow.

"Quickly!" exclaimed Hattie. "Grab hold of my tail."

Before he became too cold to move again, Hoglet managed to haul himself up to grab the tip of Hattie's tail.

"Hold on tight," she said, carrying Hoglet to where the rest of the herd waited. "I'm sure Baxter will be able to help."

Hoglet had never seen an animal as big as Baxter before; absolutely enormous with a wonderfully thick coat, he didn't seem to notice the wind and snow. Unlike Hoglet, who still couldn't feel his nose or any of his paws, Baxter appeared to be enjoying the freezing temperatures.

"This young hedgehog's trying to get to Second Chance House," said Hattie. "It's not far from here, but he's having trouble getting through the snow. Do you think you could clear a path for him?"

"Of course," said Baxter. "I'd be delighted."

Hoglet let go of Hattie's tail as the rest of the cows gathered round to keep him warm. They all watched in silence as Baxter put his head to the ground and strode forward into the driving wind. The two enormous horns on either side of his head pushed the snow aside effortlessly, and within minutes a pathway had been cleared for Hoglet to reach the edge of the field by the road.

"Oh thank you *so* much everyone," he said.

"You're welcome, but you'd best be on your way," said Hattie, "the weather's closing in."

The herd watched as Hoglet set off along the path that Baxter had cleared for him, but he hadn't gone far before he started feeling a bit wobbly and breathless.

"Oh dear," he said quietly to himself, "I'm not so sure I can manage this after all, but I can't give up after all the trouble the cows have gone to." He thought he could hear his heartbeat thumping in his ears, but then realised that it was the sound of Baxter's giant hoofs coming up beside him. The old bull lowered his head to where Hoglet was standing.

"Here," he said. "Climb up and I'll give you a lift."

Hoglet didn't find it easy clambering onto Baxter's head, and he was sure that he accidentally stuck one of his back legs up his nose, but Baxter didn't seem to mind! Eventually, the little bald hedgehog sat on the thick clump of fur right between Baxter's horns and they reached the edge of the field in no time.

"I'm afraid I can't take you any further," said Baxter, carefully lifting his head over the edge of the fence. He stayed absolutely still while Hoglet climbed down from his

head onto the grass verge at the side of the road. "I don't know anything about crossing roads," he continued, "but I do know they are dangerous, so please be careful."

"I will, I promise," replied Hoglet. "I can't thank you enough for all your help."

"You're more than welcome. Good luck, wee chap."

10. Don't Roll Up!

Hoglet crouched by the roadside thinking about all the advice the other animals had given him. Both the mouse and the robin had told him that he would have to be careful, and his mother had simply told him to stay away from roads and only cross them if he really had to.

"Oh, I wish Second Chance House was on *this* side of the road," he said, looking nervously across to the other side.

"Right, I'd better get on with it." Hoglet checked one last time to make sure there

was nothing coming, then took a deep breath and ran as fast as he could. He got halfway across, but coming towards him was the biggest, brightest set of lights he'd ever seen, like a pair of monster's eyes. His mother's advice echoed in his head: "Be brave. You'll be all right. Stay away from roads." The monster came closer and closer, and was only moments away when Hoglet suddenly remembered one other thing his mother had told him and his brother and sisters: "If you're ever on a road, you *must* keep moving. Whatever you do, don't stop and *don't* roll into a ball." Hoglet wanted desperately to roll up and hide but he trusted his mother's advice. Gritting his teeth, he shut his eyes and carried on running. There was an almighty roar. Everything went black. Then silence.

Hoglet lay in the gutter. If anyone had been around they wouldn't have noticed him, as he looked like a lump of grey slush.

11. Hope at Last

"I made it," Hoglet said quietly, still catching his breath. "I crossed the road and I'm still alive. I'm going to get to Second Chance House after all!"

He staggered out of the sludgy, murky puddle at the roadside and onto the grass verge. Looking across to the other side he saw the relieved faces of Hattie, Baxter and the rest of the Highland cattle as they realised he was alive. Their huge heads swayed from side to side in delight.

"Goodbye everyone and thanks again," he called. Hoglet watched as the herd headed back towards the middle of their field, Baxter's tail swishing happily as he ambled away into the distance.

Hoglet felt so lucky that he'd met the Highland cows and managed to cross the road safely, that he forgot about his bad leg, the cuts on his skin and his empty tummy. It was still snowing heavily but he knew he didn't have far to go now. Ahead of him he could see the small lane that the mouse and robin had told him about.

There were plenty of bushes around so it was quite easy for him to find patches of ground that the snow hadn't yet managed to cover.

"Won't be long now," he said, and as he turned into the lane he saw what he'd waited so long to see. "That must be it!"

he said to himself excitedly. "There's the line of Scots Pines. Second Chance House is at the end of this road."

By the time Hoglet set off on the final stage of his journey along the driveway it had stopped snowing. He saw a sign which read SECOND CHANCE HOUSE

and a welcoming light shone from a window up ahead.

Hoglet kept to the middle of the driveway where it was easier to walk. "I should be quite safe because the lane's surrounded by trees," he said to himself. But something was bothering him and an eerie silence hung in the air. He stopped and looked around. "Don't be silly," he told himself. "There's nothing there."

As he went further along the drive Hoglet had a horrible feeling that *someone* or *something* was watching him. Ahead of him he noticed large blobs of snow falling through the air, and then a large lump of the cold, white mixture landed on his head. He looked up. "Oh no!" he cried. In the tree above him sat a large eagle. It leaned over the branch to get a

better look at Hoglet and cocked its head
to one side.

"And just where do you think you're
going?" asked the bird.

Hoglet looked up. "Second Chance House," he replied in a rather shaky voice, "to get my second chance."

"Not if I've got anything to do with it you're not," said the eagle. "I haven't eaten for days and you look rather tasty to me."

"You wouldn't want to eat me," said Hoglet. "I'm a hedgehog."

"A hedgehog? But where are your spines?"

"I haven't got any," explained Hoglet. "That's why I really need to reach Second Chance House. So, please, could you just let me be on my way?" he pleaded.

The huge bird laughed. "You must be joking," he said. "Nature's not like that. We all need to eat, you know. Didn't your mother teach you *anything*?"

Hoglet thought about his mother and

Horatio and his two sisters and wished they were there to help him. Remembering the warning the fox had given him about birds of prey having good appetites, Hoglet darted towards the safety of a clump of heather, but he was too late. The giant bird jumped into the air and hovered briefly, before swooping and grabbing Hoglet by the neck. Hoglet tried to run but it was hopeless; the snow was too deep and his back leg still too painful. As the huge creature took Hoglet further from the ground, up into the cold air, the hedgehog tried to wriggle free, hoping the eagle would drop him as the owl had done in Tumbly Wood ... but it was no use. The bird had a firm grasp of him; Hoglet could feel its beak biting into his skin.

When all seemed lost, Hoglet had an idea. If he could just get the eagle to speak, perhaps it would drop him. "Where are you taking me?" he asked. It didn't work. They kept flying higher and higher. Hoglet was beginning to feel sick and everything was spinning round. "Are you going to eat me?" he asked.

"Of course I ..." but before the bird had time to finish its sentence Hoglet found himself falling through the air, going down, down, down. He rolled himself up tightly and shut his eyes before plunging into a mound of snow. Knowing the eagle would still be circling above, searching for him, he kept rolling deeper into the snow, making a tunnel. After a while he stopped and stayed still, protected in a little igloo.

Hoglet heard the huge bird screeching above, but he was quite safe. He unrolled himself and sat still to catch his breath. It was dark in his little snow house and very,

very cold. The only light came from the small hole above where he had landed.

He shuffled to the entrance of the igloo and poked his snout out cautiously into the cold evening air. He was relieved to hear the eagle flying away, obviously looking for an alternative meal, but the deeper he sniffed the air, the more distressed he became.

"Oh dear," he cried, "that bird must have flown for miles. I can't smell the Scots Pine trees any more." Hoglet peered hard into the dim light, but it had started snowing again, making it difficult to see anything. He inched a little further out of his igloo and had a more thorough look around, hoping against hope that he might see the welcoming light of Second Chance House, that he'd almost reached only minutes before ... but that was gone too. Then he noticed something else and squealed in despair. There, in the distance, he could just make out a signpost. He squinted, trying to get his eyes to focus more clearly.

"Oh no, I'm completely lost," he wailed. "I'm not at Second Chance House any more. That sign says I'm at END HOUSE."

Now that Hoglet had lost all hope of reaching Margaret Love, he started to notice just how cold it was. He stood outside his little snow house, shuffling from foot to foot, trying to avoid putting each of his paws in the freezing snow for too long.

"I suppose I'll just have to go back inside and wait for the snow to stop," he said, crawling back into the snow tunnel.

He turned round and round in his

little burrow, trying to get comfortable, but it was impossible. Small, freezing drops of water started falling from the ceiling onto his back, making him more miserable than he'd ever been.

"I'll never reach Second Chance House now."

His thoughts turned to his family, Horatio, Heather and Holly.

"I expect they're all hibernating safely for winter," he sighed.

Then he thought about his mother. Large tears filled his eyes as he remembered her.

"I had hoped to see her again one day, but it's obviously not meant to be," he sobbed.

Hoglet tried to remember everything his mother had taught him: always be polite, always stay under cover, stay away from foxes and badgers, never drink cows' milk, and never go to sleep in the snow, however tired you feel."

"Oh gosh," sighed Hoglet, "somehow or other I *must* stay awake or I'm going to freeze to death."

His thoughts were interrupted by a

sudden crunching noise in the snow above him. "Oh dear, oh dear," he said. "That can't be good ... the roof seems to be caving ..."

Hoglet didn't finish his sentence. He didn't see the small avalanche which landed on him, smothering him completely. Neither did he see that the only hole providing him with air and light had just been completely blocked off.

It was perhaps just as well that he didn't realise all these things, for Hoglet had, in fact, been buried alive.

12. A Warming Tail

McCavity looked up sleepily as he heard his owner's voice.

"I don't remember seeing this much snow since you were a puppy, McCavity," said Margaret Love. "And that was over ten years ago ... when you still had teeth!" She patted the large dog as he stretched out in front of a blazing coal fire.

"I'll just finish my cup of tea," continued the old lady. "Then we'd better feed the ducks and give you a quick walk before it gets any colder."

Mrs Love gave the last piece of her Highland shortbread finger to McCavity and headed through to the kitchen with her cup and saucer. After taking a generous scoop of duck food from her larder, she popped it into a plastic bag and put on her Wellington boots and cosy jacket. McCavity was on her heels, keen to have his final walk of the day.

"We'll feed the ducks first," said Margaret, "and then we'll go round the field as usual."

The old dog followed his mistress obediently as she ushered the ducks into their house for the night and left them with their supper. Then as he stood in the doorway of the little wooden house, McCavity stuck his nose in the air, sniffed frantically and suddenly shot off in the direction of the driveway to Second Chance House.

"Where on earth is he off to?" muttered the old lady. She stood outside the duck house and watched her elderly dog as he tore along the drive, stopping occasionally to sniff the air and change direction. It had stopped snowing now and although there was very little light, the moon lit the snow and she could see him rummaging around. "Silly old thing!" she said, smiling to herself. "I expect he's found a rabbit."

"Come on McCavity ... this way!" she called, but the dog refused to move and started digging furiously. Margaret started walking towards him, just as he produced a small, round, grey object from underneath a mound of snow.

"Oh, you are a clever chap!" greeted his mistress. "You've found another old tennis ball." The dog deposited it at her feet. "That's very kind of you, but I don't want it, thank you," giggled the old lady. "Come on, we'd better get home." Still McCavity refused to move and he started running in small circles around his mistress in an effort to stop her walking away. "Oh, very well, I'll throw the ball for you just once," she said.

Margaret Love bent down to pick up the ball but then she jumped back in alarm.

"Oh dear, what on earth have you found?" she exclaimed, peering closely at it. "Oh no!" she sighed. "It's a hedgehog. A completely bald hedgehog and the poor little chap's dead." She carefully picked up the tiny frozen body and held it in her hands. "Oh, I do wish I could have done something for him," she said sadly, "but you can't save them all, can you McCavity? Let's take him home and we'll bury him under a small tree somewhere in the garden in the morning."

"Here you are ... you were clever enough to find him, so you take him," she said. The dog carefully took the small creature from his mistress and proudly carried him with the greatest of care in his huge, toothless mouth.

"I'll be glad to get back indoors by the fire," said Margaret as they got closer to the house. "And look at this, there's been so much snow that half the letters of the house sign have been hidden and it looks as if it says END HOUSE rather than SECOND CHANCE HOUSE. It's such a pity that I couldn't have given that

little bald hedgehog a second chance; I'm afraid it really was the end for him."

She was busily clearing the blobs of snow from the sign when she heard a strange squeaking noise coming from behind her. It was McCavity. He was dribbling and had a strange, puzzled look on his face. "What on earth's the matter, old boy?" she asked. Very carefully McCavity opened his mouth as wide as it would go and gently placed the hedgehog at Margaret's feet again, only this time, IT MOVED! "Oh goodness gracious me, McCavity! The warmth of your mouth must have revived him ... he's ALIVE! Perhaps it's not quite the end for this little chap ... maybe we *can* give him a second chance after all!"

Without wasting any time Mrs Love and McCavity rushed back to the house as quickly as they could to see what, if anything, could be done for little Hoglet.

13. Hedgehog Heaven

Hoglet woke up. He wasn't cold or frightened or hungry. It was all over. He hadn't made it. *So this is what Hedgehog Heaven is like,* he thought to himself. But then he noticed that he was wrapped in a large fluffy towel on an elderly lady's lap by a blazing coal fire.

A large, friendly hand offered him a syringe of warm goat's milk. He drank it all, and just before falling asleep again he gazed at the old lady who smiled back at him. *So this is it,* he thought, as he nodded off. *I've found Second Chance House!*

The next few weeks passed in a blur of utter happiness for Hoglet. Everyday Mrs Love would change the tiny bandage on his leg and feed him kitten food. As a special treat every so often she would come home with a small tub of mealworms for him and, with each day

that passed, Hoglet felt himself becoming stronger.

Margaret Love picked him up one morning.

"Now then, little chap," she said. "Your leg's better and you're so fat that you can't quite roll up into a ball any more, but I can't let you out on your own yet; winter's arrived properly and it's far too cold."

She peered closely at Hoglet's skin. It wasn't sore and cracked any more; Mrs Love had been carefully rubbing a special blend of oils into it ever since he'd arrived at Second Chance House.

"And, of course, there is the problem of your spines," she went on. "They still haven't appeared and perhaps they never will. However ... we mustn't give up hope," she added, carefully rubbing more oil onto his skin. "Back you go ...

into your box," she said and tucked him in between thick layers of towelling. "I'm popping out. I shan't be long."

Mrs Love returned about an hour later armed with two chunky knitting needles, a ball of oatmeal-coloured wool and a bag of duck feathers. It was quiet in the kitchen, apart from the occasional snoring from McCavity and the clickety-click of the knitting needles. Hoglet spent most of the day dozing while the old lady worked, stopping only for numerous cups of tea accompanied by her favourite shortbread fingers.

Later that afternoon, Hoglet felt himself being gently lifted out of his box. After covering his skin with one final layer of special oil, Mrs Love held up a waistcoat she'd made especially for him. It had been carefully knitted and into each hole she had painstakingly stitched a duck's feather. She'd even gone to the trouble of searching along her driveway for three tiny pine cones to use as buttons!

"You've got so round and tubby, I think I should have made it a bit larger!" she exclaimed. "Right," she said firmly. "Time for you to hibernate, young man."

For one awful moment, Hoglet thought he was going to be dressed up to look like one of Margaret's ducks, but at the last minute she turned the small waistcoat inside out and the soft ends of the feathers switched magically to the inside of the outfit, leaving the pointed quills on the outside. Hoglet was amazed. The inside of the waistcoat was soft and warm, yet from the outside the quills made him look like a real hedgehog!

"There you go," she said, doing up the buttons of his new outfit. "It just fits ... with a little room to spare!" Margaret Love held Hoglet gently. "Well, little fellow. You're certainly plump enough to hibernate safely now. Come with me."

Mrs Love took Hoglet outside. He wasn't sure he wanted to go at first, but when he saw the little rabbit hutch Mrs Love had prepared for him, he was delighted. *My own little house, lined with leaves and straw,* he thought to himself happily.

For the first time in his life, Hoglet felt like a real hedgehog. "I've got little quill spines," he said, turning round and round in the leaves to make a nest for himself. He gave a huge yawn and rolled up into a ball. But this time it wasn't a miserable, cold, hungry ball. This time he was a warm, fat, happy ball!

Hoglet fell fast asleep for the rest of the winter, thinking how lucky he was to have found Second Chance House and Margaret Love.

14. Spring

Almost five months had passed. Mrs Love looked out of her kitchen window. "It's getting warmer," she said to herself. She went outside and quietly put a small bowl of cat food at one end of Hoglet's hutch, and then went back indoors to finish the washing-up.

It didn't take long for the smell of Hoglet's favourite food to drift through to his sleeping nest. His nose twitched and very slowly he began to unroll. He gave a long yawn and looked around sleepily. Remembering where he was, he stretched first his front legs, then his back legs. As he did so, he made a scrunchy noise in the leaves. It made him jump at first. "What was that noise?" he said. Turning round he saw there was no one else there.

Hoglet opened his eyes properly and had a better look at himself. "I've got leaves stuck to me," he said, "and little bits of straw."

Mrs Love was drying the dishes when she noticed Hoglet sitting at the dish of cat food. "I didn't think it would take him long to wake up once he smelled that food!" she said. Hoglet had been hibernating for almost twenty weeks and she was keen to see how he was after his long winter's sleep.

She went outside. Hoglet snuffled gently at her hand. "Wait there while I get some gloves," she said, "and we'll have a proper look at you."

Hoglet sat patiently while Margaret Love cut away the little knitted waistcoat. It didn't come off easily. Leaves and straw were stuck everywhere, tangled in the duck quills. Finally, the waistcoat came off completely and a huge smile spread across her face.

"Well I never!" she exclaimed. "Just

look at you. You're one of the prickliest hedgehogs I've ever seen. I don't think you'll be needing this jacket any more," she said.

Hoglet felt strange. Something wasn't right. He moved around, looking at himself. Then slowly it began to dawn on him. "I'm spiky!" he squealed in delight. "I've grown *my very own* spines!" Hoglet turned round and round in circles just for fun, catching as many bits as he could in his new overcoat, until at last he became so giddy he had to stop.

Margaret Love held Hoglet up high and smiled. "You're a handsome chap, aren't you? That's it," she said, "I'll call you Handsome!"

Hoglet, or rather Handsome, looked back at Mrs Love. "A proper name at last!" he thought. "My very own *proper* name!"

That night, after gluing a tiny gold bead onto one of Handsome's spines so that he would always be recognised, Mrs Love took him into the garden and placed him on the grass. "Well, there you are, Handsome," she said. "Spring has arrived at last and you're free to go. Come back and visit me, won't you? Good luck!"

Handsome looked up at Margaret Love. How could he ever thank her? She'd given him a bed for the winter, nursed him back to health and given him a proper name — everything he'd needed for his second chance.

Handsome curled himself into a ball — a very spiky ball — and rolled in a large circle at Mrs Love's feet. She laughed with delight and then watched as he headed towards a beech tree in a corner of her large garden.

Just before disappearing into the long grass Handsome turned round once more to face the old lady. She smiled. "Go on then. Go and do whatever it is hedgehogs do, and don't forget ... make the most of your second chance!"

Hog Epilogue

Margaret Love sat in the cosy lounge at the back of her cottage. It had been a chilly autumn day and a fire crackled in the grate.

"I won't get any more sewing done tonight," she said, looking at the fading light. She glanced at her watch. "Time for a cup of tea."

As she sipped her warm drink, Mrs Love thought about all the animals she'd helped that year. The fox who had lost his brush in a snare, a woodpecker with a broken beak, a nightingale who sang out of key, a mouse whose tail needed a splint after having been caught it in a mousetrap ... even a squirrel who was allergic to nuts!

"Then there was Handsome, of course. But you must take the credit for having rescued him, McCavity!" The old dog opened one eye when he heard her voice and stretched lazily in front of the fire.

Gazing through her patio windows Margaret suddenly noticed a dark shadow moving across the lawn.

"Oh ... it's a hedgehog!" she exclaimed, standing up to get a better view. As she watched, another hog appeared from the hedge by the path. Then another, and another, and another ... until six hedgehogs were advancing towards the house. They peered about nervously. They seemed to be looking for something ... or someone.

"I'd better go and investigate," she said. "Come on, McCavity!"

By the time Mrs Love had thrown on a hat and scarf, the six hedgehogs had stopped halfway up the lawn and were gathered in a small group. Mrs Love stood quietly, waiting to see what would happen. Various rustling noises came

from the direction of the hedge. They were getting louder.

"Are you there, Handsome?" she called. A proud, but rather shy father poked his snout through the leaves and she saw two bright, cheerful eyes that she remembered so well.

"Gosh, haven't you done well for yourself," she smiled. "Wait there!" Margaret Love disappeared back into the house and returned, minutes later, with a large bowl of cat food and a saucer of goat's milk.

"A treat to fatten you all up for the winter," she said, placing the food in the middle of the lawn.

She watched happily as the hedgehogs enjoyed the meal, finishing every last morsel. Then, suddenly, it was time to go. Handsome started to round up his family and nuzzle them back to the hedge.

"Find somewhere warm and safe to hibernate this year!" she called after him as he led his family back to the woods. But somehow she knew he would!

Margaret stood in the crisp autumn air with McCavity by her side, gazing into the distance. Soon all she could see was the sun reflecting off the gold bead on Handsome's back as he guided his family through the fallen leaves. Then the sun went down behind Tumbly Wood and they were gone.

Top Tips For Looking After Hedgehogs

by ~~Hoglet~~ Handsome

1. Hedgehogs usually hibernate between November and March but sometimes, like me, we are too skinny to go to sleep. Please feed us! You probably don't have any slugs, my favourite food, in your fridge, but we think meat-based cat or dog food is yummy too. We also like drinking water, but not cows milk — yuck!

2. A warm pile of leaves is a great place for hibernating, but people like to use leaves for bonfires. Please check bonfires before you light them in case one of my spiky friends is having a nooze in there.

Hedgehogs are nocturnal: we go out at night sleep in the day. If you see a hedgehog in ytime, something is probably wrong. The Hedgehog Preservation Society can tell you if it needs to be rescued. If so, take it inside, using gloves, and put it in a warm box with clean bedding, like towels or straw. If it isn't bleeding, give it a hot water bottle wrapped in a towel (but keep the bottle warm, if it goes cold it can be harmful). If you find one unhappy hoglet please check that it doesn't have brothers and sisters, like Horatio, Heather and Holly hiding nearby.

4. Hedgehogs love to eat, well, anything, but that can get us into trouble. If we put our heads in something like a yoghurt pot or a tin can we get stuck! Please clear up your litter.

5. Sometimes you will see a hedgehog sunbathing or wobbling when it walks. We do this when we get really cold, which is dangerous for us. If you see a hedgehog acting in this way then please take it inside right away and warm it up (see Top Tip 3). Then call the British Hedgehog Preservation Society.

British Hedgehog Preservation Society:

www.britishhedgehogs.org.uk

or call 01584 890 801.

The Cat Who Decided

Margaret Forrester

Illustrated by

Sandra Klaassen

Why does nobody want the mixter-maxter kitten? The stripy little cat is sent from the farm to the city and passed from owner to owner, but nobody wants to keep him.

When he moves into the tall house in Edinburgh and finds his name — Mac — he starts to make friends and has many adventures. He has found a home that he loves, but will he ever find a true friend?

www.florisbooks.co.uk

Hamish and the Wee Witch

Moira Miller

Illustrated by

Mairi Hedderwick

Hamish and Mirren live in a quiet farmhouse by a beautiful loch in Scotland. They are quite happy until one day a wee witch comes and steals milk from their cow. Can they outwit the witch and live in peace once more?

Moira Miller's characteristic wit and humour shine through in this delightful collection of stories.

www.florisbooks.co.uk